Mommy, I Love You

For Moucky and Grandad
Q.G.

Suzette © 2005, 2001 Mijade Publications—Belgium
Text and Illustration © 2005, 2001 Quentin Gréban

A publication of
Milk and Cookies Press, a division of ibooks, inc.

This book is a work of fiction.
Any resemblance to actual events or locales or persons, living or dead, is entirely coincidental.

ibooks, inc.
24 West 25th Street, 11th floor, New York, NY 10010

The ibooks, inc. World Wide Web Site address is:
http://www.ibooks.net

ISBN: 0-689-03922-0
First ibooks, inc. printing: April 2005
10 9 8 7 6 5 4 3 2 1

Editor–Dinah Dunn
Associate Editor – Robin Bader

Designed by Joe Bailey

Library of Congress Cataloging-in-Publication Data available

Manufactured in China

Quentin Gréban

Mommy, I Love You

MILK &
COOKIES
PRESS

New York
Distributed by Simon & Schuster, Inc.

Suzette is a very small ladybug with three black spots on her back. She doesn't know much, but she does know what she will be when she grows up—she will be an artist!

Suzette likes to draw the orange sky at sunset, the blue water, and any human that she encounters.

One day Suzette is sitting quietly on her daisy
when she sees a grasshopper bounce by.
She immediately begins to draw her.
But it is not easy to draw a grasshopper,
especially when she never stops moving.

The grasshopper bounces
away with big hops.
Suzette chases after her.

The grasshopper bounces very high and very far.
Soon Suzette falls behind and she turns back
to her daisy. But where is her daisy?
Suzette doesn't know. She is lost!

Suzette feels like crying. She calls for her mommy, but her mommy doesn't answer. All she hears is a rumbling storm in the distance.

The first raindrops start to fall.
Suzette, trembling, runs for shelter.
She is so tired that she slips in a puddle.
"If this was only a bad dream!" she
thinks. She closes her eyes and falls
asleep, hoping to be awakened by her
mother's sweet kisses.

The next day Suzette is found by a colony of ants. When they see the sad little ladybug, they know that something is wrong.

"What's the matter little one?" asks one of the ants.
"What are you doing here all by yourself?"
"I am lost," sobs Suzette, "and I am looking for
my mommy."

"What does your mommy look like?"
asks another ant. Suzette sighs.
"Mommy looks just like me, but she has
five spots instead of three and she
gives very sweet kisses."
Suzette takes her pencils out of her
backpack and begins to draw.

After a few attempts, Suzette draws a beautiful picture of her mommy, with five black spots.

"That's a really pretty mommy you've got there," says the ant, "but I haven't seen her anywhere."

Suzette is disappointed, but just then she sees a bumblebee busy gathering pollen.

"Excuse me, sir," she says, for she is a very polite ladybug. "I'm looking for my mommy. Have you seen her?" She shows the bumblebee her drawing.

"I like your drawing very much," says the bumblebee, buzzing loudly, "but I haven't seen your mommy."

Suzette heads for a pond.
A dragonfly is gliding over the water
on her transparent wings.
Her babies hover behind her.
"Excuse me," Suzette says.
"I'm looking for my mommy.
Have you seen her?"

The dragonfly looks at the drawing
with her big jeweled eyes.
"It's a beautiful drawing," she says, "but I
haven't seen your mommy."

A few steps away, Suzette spies a frog.
Uh-oh! Her mommy told her that frogs
love to eat little ladybugs!
Suzette cautiously inches closer.

"Please don't eat me," she says.
"I'm looking for my mommy.
 Have you seen her?"

The frog peers at Suzette
with his bulging eyes.
"You are lucky I am not hungry,"
he says, looking at the drawing.
"I haven't seen your mommy."
And saying this, he dives into the pond.

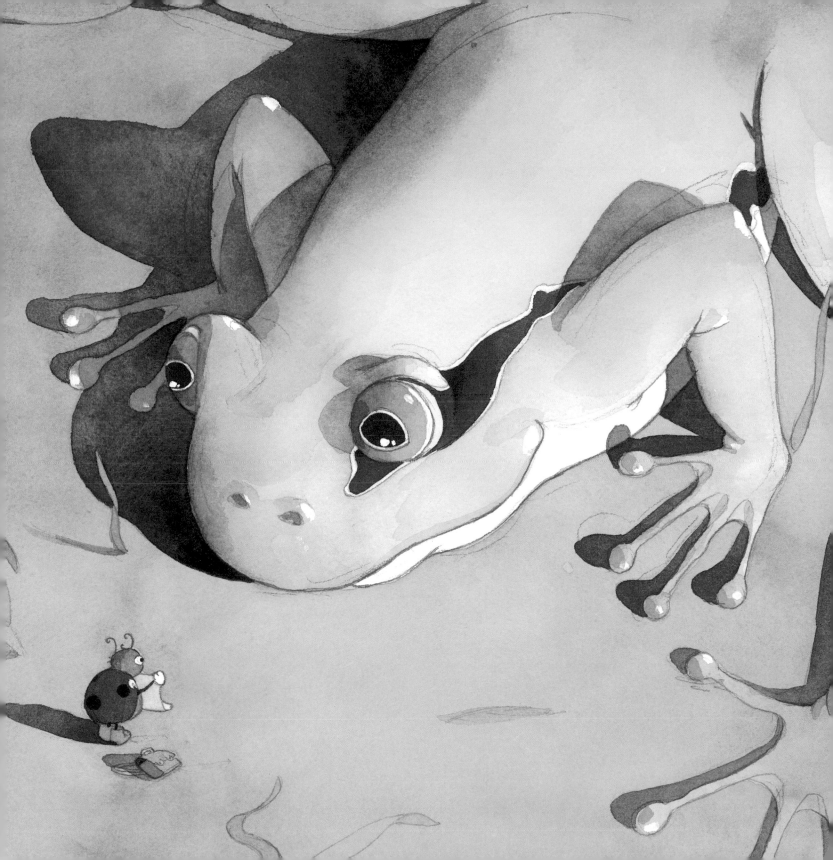

An otter pops his head out of the pond.
"Excuse me," Suzette says.
"I'm looking for my mommy. Have you seen her?"
The otter looks at Suzette's drawing.
"That is a marvelous drawing," he says.
"But I haven't seen your mommy."

Disheartened, Suzette plops
down at the foot of a mushroom.

"If only I had stayed on my daisy!" she weeps.
She looks at her drawing again and now it
doesn't look like her mommy at all!
Is that why nobody recognized her?
Suzette is so mad that she rips
the drawing to pieces.

"Oh no! I hope you haven't torn your beautiful drawing," comes a voice from behind Suzette.
She turns around and there is the ant, the bumblebee, the dragonfly, the frog, the otter—AND HER MOMMY!

Suzette jumps up and throws her arms around her mommy's neck. She holds her tight in her arms.

"Everybody recognized me from your beautiful drawing," says her mommy.

Indeed, her mommy does have five black spots on her back.

Best of all, just as Suzette
remembered, her mommy
still gives very sweet kisses.

"Mommy, I love you!" says
Suzette and they were never
apart again.